Dear Parent:
Your child's love of reading starts here!

Every child learns to read in a different way and at his or her own speed. Some go back and forth between reading levels and read favorite books again and again. Others read through each level in order. You can help your young reader improve and become more confident by encouraging his or her own interests and abilities. From books your child reads with you to the first books he or she reads alone, there are I Can Read Books for every stage of reading:

SHARED READING
Basic language, word repetition, and whimsical illustrations, ideal for sharing with your emergent reader

BEGINNING READING
Short sentences, familiar words, and simple concepts for children eager to read on their own

READING WITH HELP
Engaging stories, longer sentences, and language play for developing readers

READING ALONE
Complex plots, challenging vocabulary, and high-interest topics for the independent reader

ADVANCED READING
Short paragraphs, chapters, and exciting themes for the perfect bridge to chapter books

I Can Read Books have introduced children to the joy of reading since 1957. Featuring award-winning authors and illustrators and a fabulous cast of beloved characters, I Can Read Books set the standard for beginning readers.

A lifetime of discovery begins with the magical words **"I Can Read!"**

Visit www.icanread.com for information
on enriching your child's reading experience.

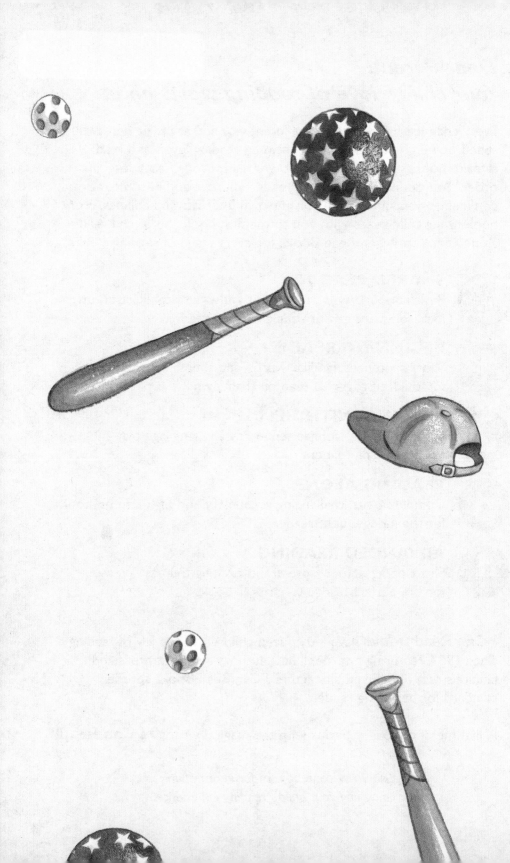

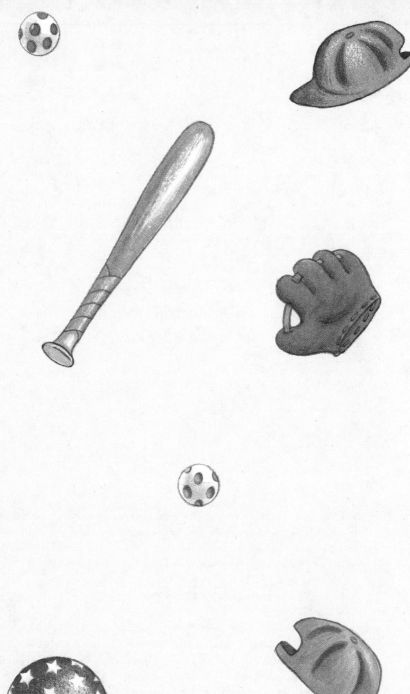

For Peter and Laura
—A.S.C.

For Alyssa,
for all the wonderful stories
that let me do what I do
—P.S.

ISBN 978-0-545-63884-5

Text copyright © 2012 by Alyssa Satin Capucilli. Illustrations copyright © 2012 by Pat Schories. All rights reserved. Published by Scholastic Inc., 557 Broadway, New York, NY 10012, by arrangement with HarperCollins Children's Books, a division of HarperCollins Publishers. I Can Read Book® is a trademark of HarperCollins Publishers. SCHOLASTIC and associated logos are trademarks and/or registered trademarks of Scholastic Inc.

20 19 18 17 16 15 14   16 17 18/0

Printed in the U.S.A.   40

First Scholastic printing, September 2013

Biscuit Plays Ball

story by ALYSSA SATIN CAPUCILLI
pictures by PAT SCHORIES

SCHOLASTIC INC.

It's time to play ball, Biscuit.

Woof, woof!

Look, Biscuit.

The game is about to begin.

Woof, woof!

Stay here now, Biscuit.

You can watch.

Woof, woof!

Wait, Biscuit.

Where are you going?

Woof!

You can't play ball now, Biscuit.

There are no dogs

in this ball game.

Stay here, Biscuit.

Woof, woof!

Uh-oh, Biscuit.

Not again!

Woof, woof!

Come along, Biscuit.
There are no dogs
in this ball game.

Won't you stay here, Biscuit?

Woof, woof!

Biscuit does not want to stay.

Woof, woof!

Biscuit wants to play, too.
Woof!

Biscuit wants to run.

Woof!

Biscuit wants to jump.
Woof!

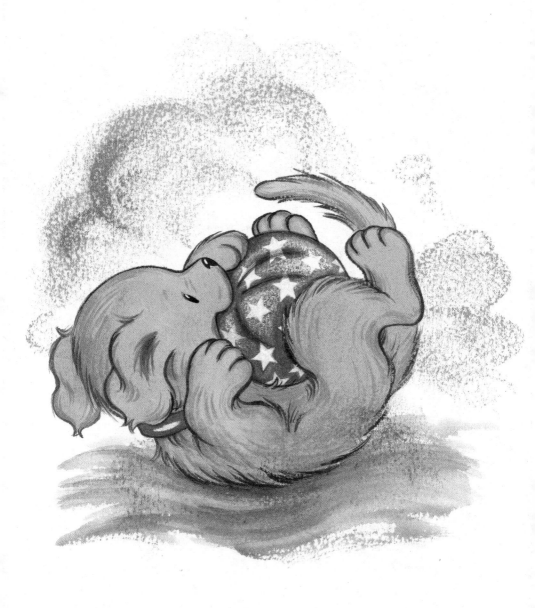

Biscuit wants to play ball!

Woof, woof!

Oh no, Biscuit.

Come back with the ball!

Silly puppy.

How can we play now?

Woof, woof! Woof, woof!

Bow wow!

Oh, Biscuit!

You found your friend Puddles.

And Puddles has a ball, too!

Woof, woof!

Bow wow!

It's time to play ball, Biscuit.

Time for all of us!

Woof!

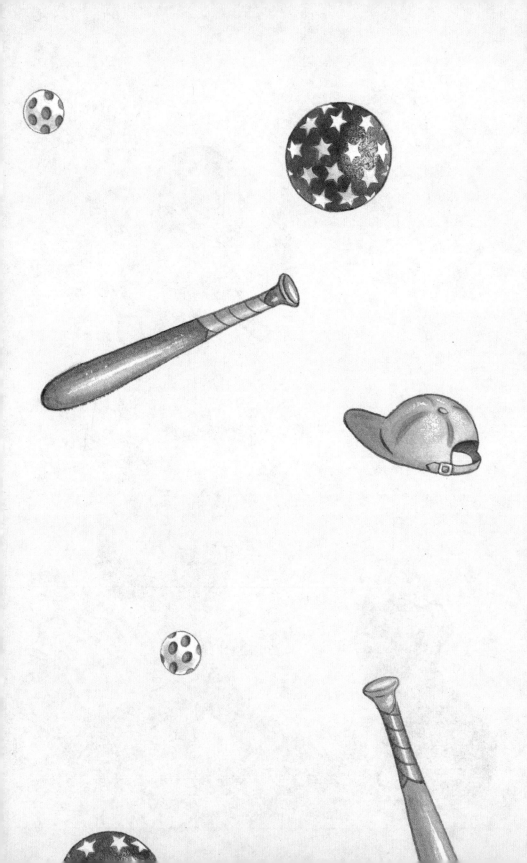

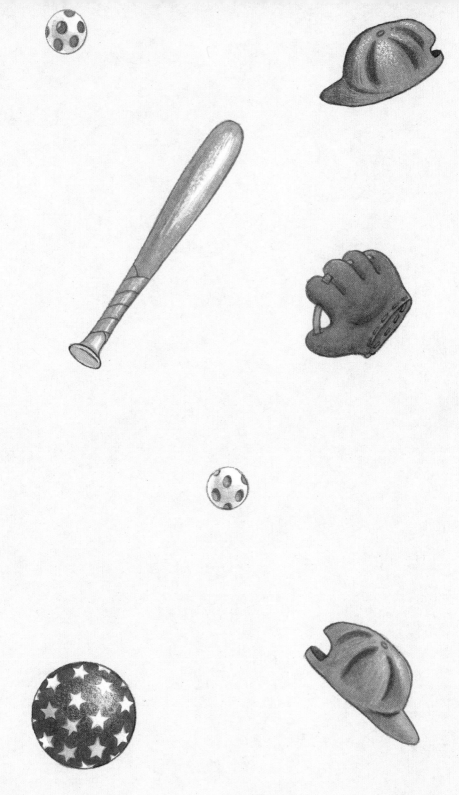